Kurious Katz and the Valentine Surprise

**Written by
Niki Mitchell**

**Photographs by
Elizabeth Roberts
and H. J. C.**

Dedicated to Marshmallow, Taffy, Snickerdoodle, and my family.

A special thanks to my readers for supporting my Kurious Katz books.

"Valentine's Day is tomorrow. Are you ready?" Taffy asked.

Marshmallow loved this holiday.

Her brain went zap. Her body went zing. Busy time!

Last year, she made a dozen cards for friends and family.

"Count me in,"
Snickerdoodle
announced.

"Me, too." Taffy never liked being left out.

"I'll ask Ned to get the art supplies," Snickerdoodle said and headed for his office.

Marshmallow's iPad rang, and she pushed the FaceTime button.

"Hey, Marshmallow," her friend, Artemis, from Happy Jack Cats, Inc., said. "Miss Emily has 25 foster cats in her care. I thought you might want to make some of your special cards."

Marshmallow's brain went zap.

Her body went zing. Volunteering time!

Twenty-five more cards would take time, but she was up for the challenge. "Of course, I'll help. So will Taffy and Snickerdoodle."

"You're the best. I'll email you the names," Artemis said before she hung up.

Marshmallow set out the glitter, paper, wiggle eyes, and scissors.

Snickerdoodle cut
a ton of hearts.

"Do you like my card?" Taffy asked.

You're a

Cool Cat!

"I like it." Marshmallow said, "I think my card looks like our friend Gus."

Be My

Valentine!

"How is this one?" Snickerdoodle asked.

"Very creative." Taffy smiled.

Marshmallow's brain went zap.
Her body went zing. Happy time!
She told Taffy and Snickerdoodle, "If we keep working this fast, we'll be done in no time."
And they kept on going.

"I went for glitter and sparkles." Marshmallow showed off her card.

"Beautiful," Snickerdoodle replied.

"Glitter is fun." Taffy made a big square that filled most of the card.

"Look at me. I'm a valentine." Snickerdoodle posed.

"Very cute." Marshmallow grabbed her iPad and snapped a picture.

It took her most of the morning to finish making cards. "Let's make catnip cookies," Taffy said.

"Grand idea," Snickerdoodle agreed, and they headed for the kitchen.

KitchenAid
The cats added ingredients like fish flakes, tuna, chicken livers, and catnip into the stand mixer. Marshmallow turned on the switch.

Snickerdoodle put two trays into the oven. Taffy set the timer for 9 minutes. Once the cookies were golden brown, they set them out to cool.

Marshmallow couldn't resist sampling one of the cookies.

Snickerdoodle and Taffy sampled treats on the floor. They saved the rest for the foster cats.

"I need a nap."
Snickerdoodle jumped on a bed and fell asleep.

"Great idea," Taffy said. He and Marshmallow found their own spots to sleep.

"An hour later, Ned brought Marshmallow, Taffy, and Snickerdoodle to Happy Jack Cats, Incorporated. He carried in the treats.

Marshmallow, Taffy, and Snickerdoodle brought in bags with cards.
Happy Valentine's Day
Happy Valentine's Day
Happy Valentine's Day

"Let's head for the cat room," Miss Emily called. Cats and kittens scattered off. "We're going through that door and to the left." She led Marshmallow, Taffy, Snickerdoodle, and Ned.

Kittens and cats were everywhere.
Count how many animals are in this picture.

Ned passed out the cookies. The Kurious Katz handed out their valentines.

"Thank you," Miss Emily said. "What you did for us was wonderful." Artemis and the other cats purred their thanks.

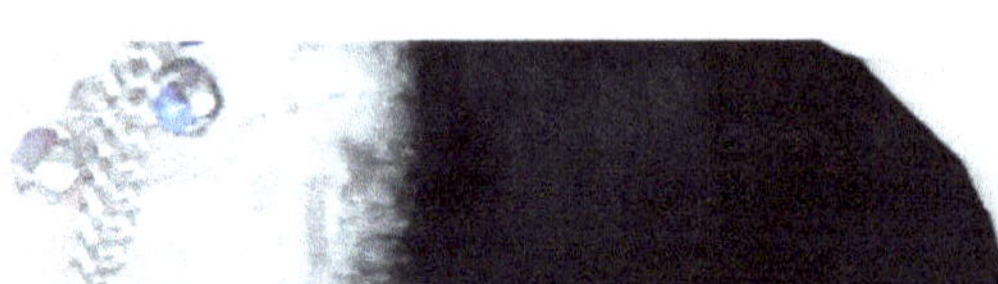

"It was our pleasure," Marshmallow said.

"I love giving to others."

"So, do I," Snickerdoodle and Taffy agreed.

Happy Valentine's Day
Marshmallow, Taffy, Snickerdoodle, and Ned!

"We made you a valentine poster. All the cats signed it by dipping their paws in paint." Hercules smiled.

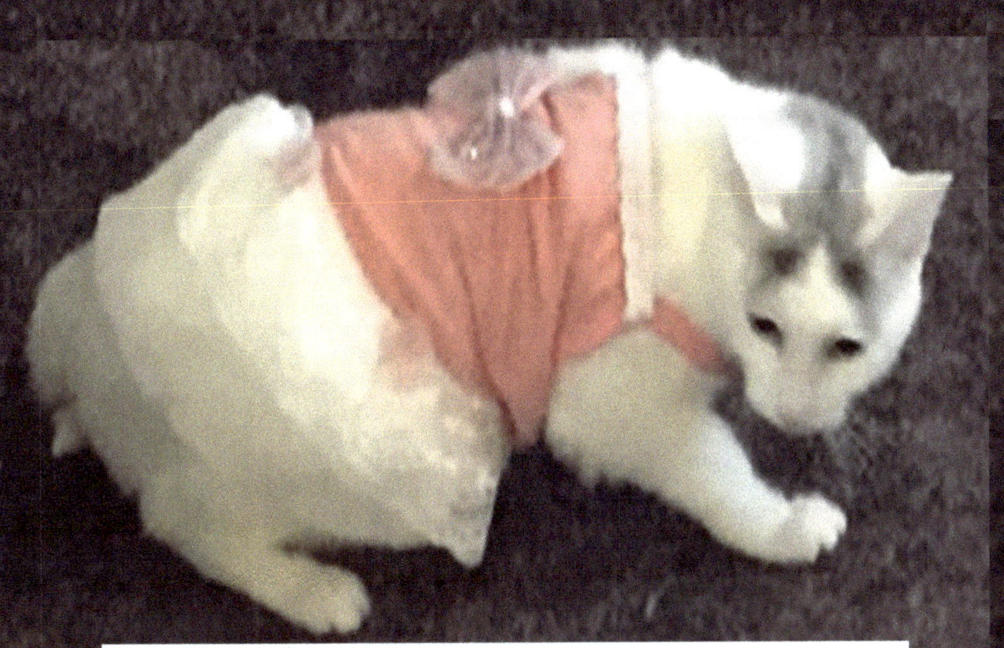

"It's purr-fect!"
Marshmallow's brain went zap.
Her body went zing.
Happy time!
Her heart filled with joy.
It was the best Valentine's Day ever.

Words to Know

added	great	saved
asleep	hearts	set
bags	holiday	she
being	hour	showed
best	how	smiled
body	I'll	Snickerdoodle
brought	jumped	Taffy
button	keep	thanks
card	liked	they
couldn't	looks	think
cute	loved	this
do	making	through
each	many	time
everyone	Marshmallow	treats
eyes	me	Valentine's Day
fast	morning	very
fell	most	very
filled	of	went
fish	office	wiggle
five	once	working
found	one	would
glitter	paper	you
grabbed	said	you're

About the Author

   Niki Mitchell is a retired teacher from Hesperia, California. The photographs are real. Her cats think everything around the house is for their enjoyment. If you enjoyed her Kurious Katz story, feedback on Facebook or Amazon would be greatly appreciated.

   She looks forward to hearing from her readers.

Website

https://kuriouskatz.weebly.com/

Facebook: Kurious Katz Author Page

https://www.facebook.com/kuriouskatzauthor/

Instagram: KuriousKatzBook

https://www.instagram.com/kuriouskatzbook/?hl=en

 # Books by Niki Mitchell

Coming Soon